Thumbelina

RETOLD BY MICHÈLE DUFRESNE · ILLUSTRATED BY GILLIAN ROBERTS

PIONEER VALLEY EDUCATIONAL PRESS, INC.

Once upon a time there was a woman who did not have any children. One day she saw a fairy and asked the fairy for help. "I wish to have a child," she told the fairy. "Can you help me?"

"Oh yes, I can help you," said the fairy. The fairy gave the woman a barleycorn seed. "Plant this barleycorn seed in a pot and see what happens."

The woman planted the barleycorn seed in a pot. Soon a flower started to grow. "Look at this beautiful flower!" said the woman, and she kissed the flower.

The flower opened up and inside
was a tiny, little girl. "You are lovely!"
exclaimed the woman. "And no bigger
than my thumb, so I will call you Thumbelina."

During the day, Thumbelina floated in a bowl of water on a boat made of a tulip leaf. Each night, she slept in a bed made from a walnut shell.

One night while Thumbelina was sleeping, a large, ugly toad jumped into her room through an open window. "You are so beautiful," said the toad. "What a pretty, little wife you will make for my son."

The toad picked up Thumbelina in the walnut shell, and he hopped out the window and off to a nearby pond.

The toad put Thumbelina on a lily pad in the pond. "You can't get away from here," he said.

Thumbelina sat on the lily pad and cried. She did not want to marry the toad's son.

Two fish swam by the lily pad.
They heard Thumbelina crying
and wanted to help her. The fish chewed and
chewed on the stem of the lily pad.
The stem broke and the lily pad began
to float away. It floated until Thumbelina
drifted far away from the toad.

All summer, Thumbelina lived alone
in the forest. Then it began to get colder
and colder. One cold, snowy day, she came
to a small door at the bottom of a tree.

A field mouse opened the door.
"Please, may I come in?" she asked, shivering.

"You poor creature. Come into my home and warm up," said the mouse. "Stay here for the winter and sing me sweet songs."

One day, a mole came to visit the mouse. After the mole heard Thumbelina's songs, he said, "Marry me. Come live in my lovely home."

Thumbelina did not want to marry the mole.

"In the spring, you must marry my friend the mole," insisted the mouse. "He is rich and will take good care of you!" Finally, Thumbelina agreed. She did not know what else to do.

One day while Thumbelina was out walking, she saw a bird lying on the path. She thought that he must be dead. Then, the bird moaned. "Are you alive, Little Bird?" Thumbelina asked.

"Yes," said the bird. "I hurt my wing on a thornbush, and I cannot fly. I am very cold."

Thumbelina got some leaves and covered the bird. Then, she brought him some water. Thumbelina took care of the bird while he grew stronger and stronger.

Thumbelina told the bird about her plans to marry the mole in the spring.

"Do not marry the mole," said the bird. "Fly away with me instead, and I will take you to a place far over the mountains where it is always summer."

"Yes! I will go with you," said Thumbelina. She climbed onto the bird's back and off they flew, high into the sky.

They flew over the mountains far, far away. Finally, they came to a beautiful valley. Thumbelina looked down and saw tiny, white flowers growing beside a lake.

The bird flew down and landed next to a large tree. Thumbelina climbed off of the bird and looked around.

"This is my home," said the bird,
showing Thumbelina a nest in the tree.
"But you should choose one of the flowers
to live in."

Thumbelina went to a flower
and saw a tiny, young man dressed in white.
He wore a gold crown and had white wings.

"Oh, look!" said Thumbelina. She thought
the young man was very handsome.

The tiny, young man took off his crown and gave it to Thumbelina. He asked her to marry him and live with him in his home in the flower.

"Yes," agreed Thumbelina. Each day, the bird sang sweet songs to Thumbelina and her handsome, young man. And everyone lived happily ever after.